GOSCINNY AND UDERZO

PRESENT

An Asterix Adventure

ASTERIX AT THE OLYMPIC GAMES

Written by RENÉ GOSCINNY *and Illustrated by* ALBERT UDERZO

Translated by Anthea Bell *and* Derek Hockridge

Asterix titles available now

1 Asterix the Gaul
2 Asterix and the Golden Sickle
3 Asterix and the Goths
4 Asterix the Gladiator
5 Asterix and the Banquet
6 Asterix and Cleopatra
7 Asterix and the Big Fight
8 Asterix in Britain
9 Asterix and the Normans
10 Asterix the Legionary
11 Asterix and the Chieftain's Shield
12 Asterix at the Olympic Games
13 Asterix and the Cauldron
14 Asterix in Spain
15 Asterix and the Roman Agent
16 Asterix in Switzerland
17 The Mansions of the Gods
18 Asterix and the Laurel Wreath
19 Asterix and the Soothsayer
20 Asterix in Corsica
21 Asterix and Caesar's Gift
22 Asterix and the Great Crossing
23 Obelix and Co.
24 Asterix in Belgium
25 Asterix and the Great Divide
26 Asterix and the Black Gold
27 Asterix and Son
28 Asterix and the Magic Carpet
29 Asterix and the Secret Weapon
30 Asterix and Obelix All at Sea
31 Asterix and the Actress
32 Asterix and the Class Act
33 Asterix and the Falling Sky
34 Asterix and Obelix's Birthday – the Golden Book

Where's Asterix?
Where's Dogmatix?
Asterix and the Vikings
Asterix at the Olympic Games (film tie-in)
Asterix Omnibus 1 (Books 1-3)
Asterix Omnibus 2 (Books 4-6)
Asterix Omnibus 3 (Books 7-9)
Asterix Omnibus 4 (Books 10-12)
Asterix Omnibus 5 (Books 13-15)
Asterix Omnibus 6 (Books 16-18)
Asterix Omnibus 7 (Books 19-21)
Asterix Omnibus 8 (Books 22-24)
Asterix Omnibus 10 (Books 28-30)
Asterix Omnibus 11 (Books 31-33)
How Obelix Fell into the Magic Potion

Original title: *Astérix aux jeux Olympiques*

Exclusive licensee: Orion Publishing Group
Translators: Anthea Bell and Derek Hockridge
Typography: Bryony Newhouse

This revised edition first published in 2004 by Orion Books Ltd,
Orion House, 5 Upper Saint Martin's Lane, London WC2H 9EA
An Hachette UK company

13 15 17 19 20 18 16 14 12

Printed in China

www.asterix.com
www.orionbooks.co.uk

A CIP record for this book is available from the British Library

ISBN 978-0-7528-6626-0 (cased)
ISBN 978-0-7528-6627-7 (paperback)

The Orion Publishing Group's policy is to use papers that are natural, renewable and recyclable products and made from wood grown in sustainable forests. The logging and manufacturing processes are expected to conform to the environmental regulations of the country of origin.

THE YEAR IS 50 BC. GAUL IS ENTIRELY OCCUPIED BY THE ROMANS. WELL, NOT ENTIRELY ... ONE SMALL VILLAGE OF INDOMITABLE GAULS STILL HOLDS OUT AGAINST THE INVADERS. AND LIFE IS NOT EASY FOR THE ROMAN LEGIONARIES WHO GARRISON THE FORTIFIED CAMPS OF TOTORUM, AQUARIUM, LAUDANUM AND COMPENDIUM ...

ASTERIX, THE HERO OF THESE ADVENTURES. A SHREWD, CUNNING LITTLE WARRIOR, ALL PERILOUS MISSIONS ARE IMMEDIATELY ENTRUSTED TO HIM. ASTERIX GETS HIS SUPERHUMAN STRENGTH FROM THE MAGIC POTION BREWED BY THE DRUID GETAFIX . . .

OBELIX, ASTERIX'S INSEPARABLE FRIEND. A MENHIR DELIVERY MAN BY TRADE, ADDICTED TO WILD BOAR. OBELIX IS ALWAYS READY TO DROP EVERYTHING AND GO OFF ON A NEW ADVENTURE WITH ASTERIX – SO LONG AS THERE'S WILD BOAR TO EAT, AND PLENTY OF FIGHTING. HIS CONSTANT COMPANION IS DOGMATIX, THE ONLY KNOWN CANINE ECOLOGIST, WHO HOWLS WITH DESPAIR WHEN A TREE IS CUT DOWN.

GETAFIX, THE VENERABLE VILLAGE DRUID, GATHERS MISTLETOE AND BREWS MAGIC POTIONS. HIS SPECIALITY IS THE POTION WHICH GIVES THE DRINKER SUPERHUMAN STRENGTH. BUT GETAFIX ALSO HAS OTHER RECIPES UP HIS SLEEVE . . .

CACOFONIX, THE BARD. OPINION IS DIVIDED AS TO HIS MUSICAL GIFTS. CACOFONIX THINKS HE'S A GENIUS. EVERYONE ELSE THINKS HE'S UNSPEAKABLE. BUT SO LONG AS HE DOESN'T SPEAK, LET ALONE SING, EVERYBODY LIKES HIM . . .

FINALLY, VITALSTATISTIX, THE CHIEF OF THE TRIBE. MAJESTIC, BRAVE AND HOT-TEMPERED, THE OLD WARRIOR IS RESPECTED BY HIS MEN AND FEARED BY HIS ENEMIES. VITALSTATISTIX HIMSELF HAS ONLY ONE FEAR, HE IS AFRAID THE SKY MAY FALL ON HIS HEAD TOMORROW. BUT AS HE ALWAYS SAYS, TOMORROW NEVER COMES.

IT IS LATE SPRING AND EVERYTHING IS PEACEFUL IN THE LITTLE GAULISH VILLAGE WE KNOW SO WELL. OBELIX AND HIS APPRENTICE, DOGMATIX, ARE OUT DELIVERING MENHIRS, ASTERIX IS SUNBATHING OUTSIDE HIS HUT, PEOPLE LAZE ABOUT ENJOYING A SIESTA. YES, BY TOUTATIS, THE LITTLE GAULISH VILLAGE IS VERY PEACEFUL...

WHEREAS THE ROMAN CAMP OF AQUARIUM SEEMS TO BE IN A STATE OF GREAT EXCITEMENT ...
GOOD OLD CAESAR!
BY JUPITER!
GOOD OLD GLUTEUS!
BY MERCURY!
YOU'LL NEVER RUN ALONE!
?

WHAT'S ALL THE NOISE ABOUT?
A MESSENGER HAS JUST COME FROM ROME WITH THE GOOD NEWS. GLUTEUS MAXIMUS HAS BEEN SELECTED TO REPRESENT ROME AT THE OLYMPIC GAMES!

GLUTEUS MAXIMUS? WHO'S HE?
YOU'RE PRETTY GREEN, AREN'T YOU, BILIUS? GLUTEUS MAXIMUS IS OUR CHAMPION! HE'S ONE OF OUR GARRISON, AND A CREDIT TO US ALL!

O GLUTEUS MAXIMUS, HOW RIGHT I WAS TO SEND YOU TO ROME FOR THE TRIALS! YOU'VE BEEN SELECTED, ALONG WITH THE BEST ATHLETES OF THE WHOLE ROMAN WORLD!
WELL, THAT'S NOT SURPRISING O CENTURION GAIUS VERIAMBITIUS. I'M THE GREATEST!

I WAS NEAR AQUARIUM PICKING MUSHROOMS – THEY'RE GOOD OVER THERE – WHEN I HEARD CHEERING. THE ROMANS SEEM TO BE IN A VERY GOOD MOOD!
SQUAWK! CLUCK!

HM... THAT'S ODD, GERIATRIX. I DON'T KNOW WHAT TO MAKE OF THEM...

SOUP. MUSHROOM SOUP IS VERY NICE.
?

SOUP?!... IS THAT ALL YOU CAN THINK OF, OBELIX?!...

WHEN YOU GET MUSHROOMS YOU SHOULD MAKE AN OMELETTE. THAT'S HOW THE REAL GOURMET EATS THEM!
2A

BUT, CHIEF VITALSTATISTIX...
NOT ANOTHER WORD – I DO THE ORDERING ROUND HERE! WE'LL HAVE AN OMELETTE!
I WAS THINKING ... PERHAPS ON TOAST...

SOMETIMES I GET THE IMPRESSION OUR FRIENDS DON'T TAKE THINGS SERIOUSLY ENOUGH... IT MAY BE A BAD SIGN FOR US IF THE ROMANS ARE IN A GOOD MOOD.
SO WHAT DO YOU SUGGEST, O DRUID?

LET THEM STEW IN THEIR OWN JUICE!

IT BRINGS OUT THE FLAVOUR.
?!?
2B

AT AQUARIUM, WHILE THE DUTY BUCCINIST IS BLOWING 'COME TO THE COOK-HOUSE DOOR, BOYS'...
TARATATARIII

A MORE SOPHISTICATED BLOW-OUT HAS BEEN PROVIDED FOR LEGIONARY GLUTEUS MAXIMUS.
HERE'S YOUR SUPPER. I HOPE IT WILL DO.

NOT BAD, O CENTURION GAIUS VERIAMBITIUS. ARMY RATIONS ARE IMPROVING! WHAT ARE THESE LITTLE BLACK THINGS?
THEY'RE STURGEON'S EGGS, SENT FROM PERSIA TO OUR COMMANDING OFFICER – CAVIAR TO THE GENERAL, SO TO SPEAK!

IF YOU WIN THE GOLD PALM AT THE OLYMPIC GAMES THERE'LL BE EXTRA PASSES FOR THE CIRCUS AND PROMOTION ALL ROUND.

SPORTING PRESTIGE IS A MATTER OF SUCH NATIONAL IMPORTANCE THAT IF YOU WIN I COULD EVEN BECOME PREFECT OF GAUL! DON'T LET ME DOWN!
STOP WORRYING – I WON'T FAIL YOU, VERIAMBITIUS.
3A

IT'LL BE A PUSHOVER. I'M THE GREATEST! NOW I'M OFF TO THE FOREST TO DO SOME TRAINING.

HIS MORALE IS MARVELLOUS. WITH CONFIDENCE LIKE THAT, HE CAN'T LOSE!

FIRST A BIT OF SPRINTING – I'M THE FASTEST MAN IN THE WORLD!

MEANWHILE, IN ANOTHER PART OF THE FOREST...
I FEEL ON TOP FORM FOR A SPOT OF BOAR-HUNTING. GETAFIX GAVE ME SOME OF THE MAGIC POTION WHICH MAKES US INVINCIBLE!
I KNOW, I KNOW, AND I DIDN'T GET ANY SEEING AS I...

ONE! TWO! ONE! TWO!
?!?
3B

WHAT'S THE MATTER WITH THAT ROMAN?
I HAVEN'T A CLUE. PERHAPS SOMEONE'S AFTER HIM.

I'LL GO AND ASK HIM.
!
?

ONE! TWO! I'M THE FASTEST! ONE!...
EXCUSE ME...

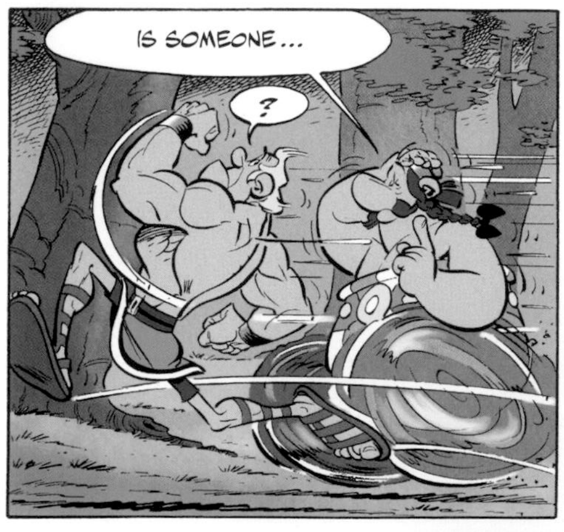
IS SOMEONE...
?

...AFTER YOU?
!
OBELIX!

LEAVE THAT ROMAN ALONE...
!
4A

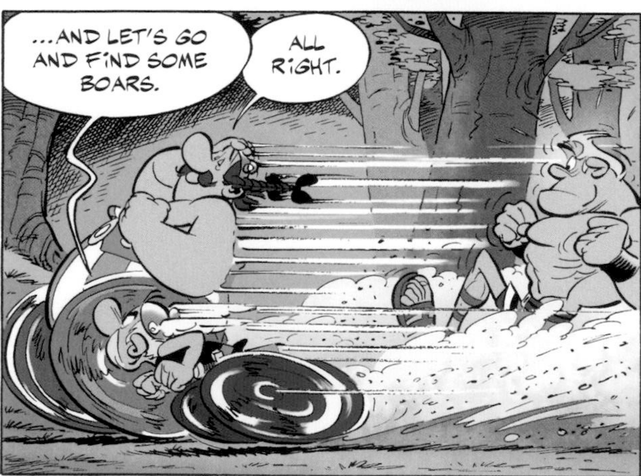
...AND LET'S GO AND FIND SOME BOARS.
ALL RIGHT.

THEY OVERTOOK ME! BOTH OF THEM!

ANYWAY, WHEN IT COMES TO THROWING THE JAVELIN...
CRACK!

I'M THE GREATEST!

PAAAF!
4B

DON'T TAKE ANY NOTICE OF MY FRIEND, ROMAN...

OBELIX! WHY DID YOU DO THAT? HE WASN'T BOTHERING US.
WHAT D'YOU MEAN? HE THREW THAT BIT OF WOOD AT MY HEAD, SO I THREW ONE BACK AT HIM. WE'RE QUITS NOW.
SNIFF SNIFF

YOU'RE NOT GOING TO GET AWAY WITH THIS, BY JUPITER!

YOU, FATTY! I'LL TAKE YOU ON AT ORDINARY WRESTLING, ALL-IN WRESTLING, BOXING! I'LL WALLOP YOU AT THOSE! I'M THE GREATEST! I'M...

I'M NOT FAT!
PAFFF!

TELL ME STRAIGHT, ASTERIX, ONCE AND FOR ALL: DO YOU THINK I'M FAT?
OF COURSE NOT, OBELIX. YOUR CHEST HAS SLIPPED A BIT, THAT'S ALL. COME ON, ARE WE GOING TO GET THOSE BOARS?

I'M HOPELESS!

WHAT D'YOU MEAN, HOPELESS?!?

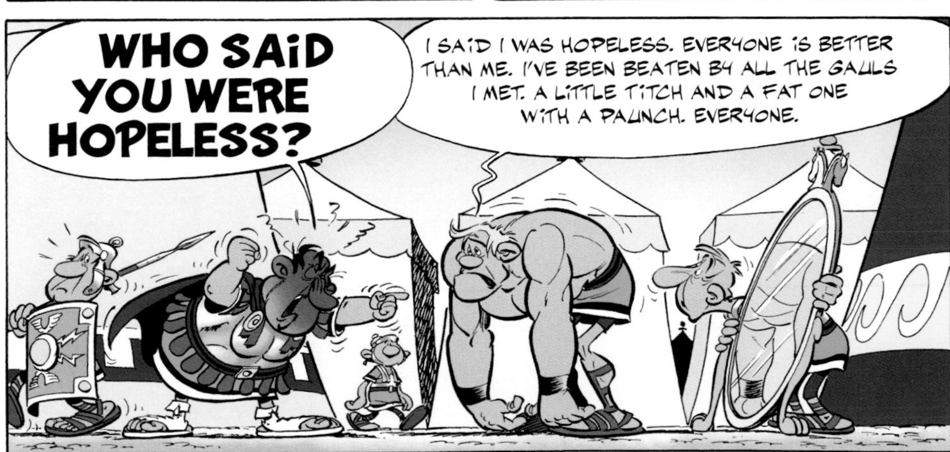
WHO SAID YOU WERE HOPELESS?
I SAID I WAS HOPELESS. EVERYONE IS BETTER THAN ME. I'VE BEEN BEATEN BY ALL THE GAULS I MET. A LITTLE TITCH AND A FAT ONE WITH A PAUNCH. EVERYONE.

THE GAULS, BY JUPITER! IT'S BEEN A LONG TIME SINCE WE HAD ANY TROUBLE WITH THEM!

BACK TO YOUR TENT, CHAMP. HAVE A REST.
I'M NOT A CHAMP. I'M HOPELESS.

I'M GOING ON FATIGUES. I WANT A BROOM – NOT TOO HEAVY.

AND I'M GOING TO SEE THESE GAULS.

THE ENTRY OF CENTURION GAIUS VERAMBITIUS INTO THE GAULISH VILLAGE DOES NOT GO UNNOTICED.
FANCY THAT! A ROMAN.

TAKE ME TO YOUR LEADER.
HE'S BUSY.
6A

TELL HIM IT'S URGENT! OFFICIAL BUSINESS!
ALL RIGHT, ALL RIGHT, KEEP YOUR HAIR ON. THE SKY ISN'T FALLING ON ANYONE'S HEAD!

IT'S ALWAYS THE SAME! SOMEONE COMES AND DISTURBS ME WHEN I'M IN MY BATH. LAST YEAR, AND THE YEAR BEFORE THAT; IT NEVER FAILS!

VERY WELL. SINCE IT'S AN OFFICIAL VISIT, LET'S OBSERVE THE CORRECT PROTOCOL.

!!!
6B

I'M LISTENING, O ROMAN!
IT'S LIKE THIS: ONE OF MY MEN HAS BEEN SELECTED TO REPRESENT MY GARRISON AT THE OLYMPIC GAMES...

...AND SOME OF YOUR GAULS, ENTIRELY UNPROVOKED, HAVE GONE AND PUT HIM OFF HIS STRIDE!

ALL I ASK IS THAT HE SHOULD BE ALLOWED TO TRAIN IN PEACE.
I'LL THINK ABOUT IT, ROMAN, AND I'LL LET YOU HAVE MY ANSWER.

CHEERIO!
AVE!

THIS IS IMPORTANT! IMPEDIMENTA! MY CLOTHES! I'LL FINISH MY BATH NEXT YEAR. PUT ME DOWN, YOU TWO, AND DON'T SPILL ANYTHING!

SOON AFTERWARDS...
WHAT EXACTLY ARE THE OLYMPIC GAMES?
THE SACRED GAMES, INCLUDING TRACK AND FIELD EVENTS, ARE HELD UNDER THE AEGIS OF ZEUS. THEY TAKE PLACE EVERY FOUR YEARS, AT OLYMPIA IN GREECE, WHERE THE HELLENES LIVE, IN THE MONTH OF HECATOMBEON.*
* JULY-AUGUST

THESE GAMES CONSTITUTE A SACRED TRUCE AND LAST FOR FIVE DAYS. GREAT IS THE GLORY OF THE VICTOR AND HIS PEOPLE!

CHIEF, WE'LL HAVE TO COOK SOMETHING UP!
I KNOW WHAT!

MUSHROOM SOUP!
?

I'M TELLING YOU! THEY WON'T WORRY YOU ANY MORE. COME ON, BE A GOOD CHAP, PUT THAT BROOM DOWN!
NO, EVEN THIS BROOM IS TOO GOOD FOR ME!

ALL RIGHT, JUST SUPPOSE THEY ARE BETTER THAN YOU, IT'S ONLY BECAUSE THEY'VE GOT A MAGIC POTION WHICH GIVES THEM SUPERHUMAN STRENGTH – THAT'S ALL!

YOUR OPPONENTS AT THE GAMES WON'T HAVE ANY POTION! HO! HO! HO!
THAT'S TRUE! I HADN'T THOUGHT OF THAT!
CENTURION, A GAULISH CHIEF WOULD LIKE TO SEE YOU.

SPLENDID! I'LL SHOW THEM I'M FRIENDLY BY OBSERVING THEIR OWN CUSTOMS. THAT WILL FLATTER THEM. MY HELMET! WHERE'S MY HELMET?

SOON AFTERWARDS...
O GAUL, THE CENTURION WILL SEE YOU OUTSIDE HIS TENT!
YOU HEARD, BOYS! IN WE GO!

WOTCHER!
AVE!

I'VE BEEN THINKING ABOUT WHAT YOU SAID...
AND?

WE'VE DECIDED TO ENTER FOR THE OLYMPIC GAMES AS WELL!
WHAT?

YES, WE'LL SEND A CHAMPION TO OLYMPIA! AND MAY THE BEST MAN WIN! CHEERIO!
WHOOSH! WHOOSH! WHOOSH! WHOOSH!

WAIT A MINUTE, GAUL! WAIT!
HANG ON, BOYS.

YOU CAN'T ENTER FOR THE OLYMPIC GAMES! THEY'RE RESERVED EXCLUSIVELY FOR GREEKS – FREE HELLENIC CITIZENS. THE ONLY OUTSIDERS ALLOWED ARE ROMANS. YOU GAULS CAN'T GO!

YOU'RE NOT HAVING ME ON?

YOU FIND OUT, GAUL, AND YOU'LL SEE I'M ON THE LEVEL.

THERE YOU ARE, GLUTEUS MAXIMUS! FEELING BETTER NOW?
FEELING BETTER? ...

I'LL GET STRAIGHT BACK INTO TRAINING, BY JUPITER!

SOON AFTERWARDS...
THAT ROMAN'S QUITE RIGHT. I HADN'T THOUGHT OF IT. ONLY GREEKS AND ROMANS HAVE THE RIGHT TO ENTER THE SACRED GAMES.

BUT, BY TOUTATIS...

...WE ARE ROMANS!

US, ROMANS? SINCE WHEN?
SINCE OLD JULIUS CONQUERED GAUL! HE'S COMMENTED ON THE SUBJECT AT LENGTH, HASN'T HE?
AM I A ROMAN?
OF COURSE! ASTERIX IS RIGHT. WE'RE PART OF THE ROMAN WORLD!

LET'S ORGANIZE A FEAST TO CELEBRATE. SOME PEOPLE ARE GOING TO GET A SURPRISE!

IN THE CAMP OF AQUARIUM...
I SHOULDN'T BE SURPRISED IF THOSE GAULS WERE UP TO SOMETHING...

...I DON'T TRUST THEM AN INCH...

I THINK I'LL GO AND SCOUT ROUND NEAR THEIR VILLAGE.
10A

CARRY ON TRAINING, GLUTEUS MAXIMUS. I'LL BE BACK SOON.
NEXT!
PAF!
JOIN THE ARMY, THEY SAID. AN ATMOSPHERE OF HEALTHY COMRADESHIP, THEY SAID...

SOON AFTERWARDS...
I'LL TAKE A PEEP THROUGH THAT CRACK OVER THERE...

WE'RE ROMANS!
UP WITH US ROMANS!

THESE ROMANS ARE CRAZY!

I ASK YOU! YOU FIGHT PEOPLE, YOU MASSACRE THEM, YOU INVADE AND OCCUPY THEIR TERRITORY, AND THEN THEY TURN AGAINST YOU FOR NO REASON AT ALL!
10B

ET NUNC, REGES, INTELLIGITE...

...ERUDIMINI, QUI JUDICATIS TERRAM.
EVERYTHING UNDER CONTROL, CENTURION?

???

!

IN THE GAULISH VILLAGE, MORALE IS HIGH...
SCRUNCH! SCRUNCH!
WITH THE MAGIC POTION TO MAKE US INVINCIBLE, WE'RE SURE TO WIN! THAT'S WHAT I CALL SPORT – NOTHING LEFT TO CHANCE!
THAT REMINDS ME, WE MUST SELECT THE CHAMPIONS TO REPRESENT OUR VILLAGE.
11A

COME ALONG! EVERYONE TAKE HIS MAGIC POTION BEFORE THE HEATS!

ON YOUR MARKS! THE FINISHING LINE IS OVER THERE, BY CACOFONIX.
HE SAID EVERYONE.
NOT YOU, OBELIX. YOU FELL IN IT WHEN YOU WERE A BABY!

SELECTION PROVES DIFFICULT, SINCE ALL THE COMPETITORS HAVE MAGIC POTION COMING OUT OF THEIR EARS, THEY ALL SHOW THE SAME TURN OF SPEED.
I MIGHT HAVE KNOWN YOU'D SAY THAT!
SHUT UP! AND RUN!
BRATS! LET YOUR ELDERS AND BETTERS PASS!
YOUTH MUST HAVE ITS FLING!
BADABOOMBADABOOMBADABOOM

WANT A POKE UP YOUR HOOTER?
GRANDPA!
11B

THE OLDEST INHABITANT SHOULD REPRESENT THE VILLAGE!
NO! I SHALL GO TO THE OLYMPIC GAMES!

HUH! MIGHT JUST AS WELL SEND DOGMATIX. HE'S BETTER THAN YOU.
BETTER THAN ME?

WELL, CAN YOU SCRATCH YOUR EAR WITH YOUR HIND LEG?
?!

ORDER! ORDER! THE OLYMPIC COMMITTEE HAS CHOSEN OUR TEAM.

ASTERIX, BECAUSE HE'S THE MOST INTELLIGENT AND BECAUSE WITHOUT HIM WE WOULDN'T BE COMPETING IN THE GAMES AT ALL, AND OBELIX, BECAUSE THE POTION HAD A PERMANENT EFFECT ON HIM.
12A

EXACTLY! I FELL IN WHEN I WAS A BABY!
GET AWAY! DO TELL ME ALL ABOUT IT...

AND NOW, I'VE GOT A SURPRISE FOR YOU! WE SHALL ALL ACCOMPANY OUR TEAM TO OLYMPIA TO CHEER THEM ON!
GOOD OLD VITALSTATISTIX!
GOOD OLD ASTERIX!
GOOD OLD OBELIX!

?
OBJECTION! I DON'T AGREE! LOOK!
? ? ? ? ? ? ? ? ? ? ? ?

!!!!
12B

AS THE DAY OF DEPARTURE APPROACHES, MORALE IN THE ROMAN CAMP IS GOING DOWN AND DOWN ...

...WHEREAS IN THE GAULISH VILLAGE EVERYONE IS IN THE BEST OF SPIRITS. CHIEF VITALSTATISTIX IS PLANNING THE JOURNEY...
I'VE HIRED A BOAT. WE'RE GOING TO BE VERY COMFORTABLE: ONE CLASS ONLY, DECK GAMES, OPEN AIR SPORTS AND MARVELLOUS ATMOSPHERE!

THE DRUID GETAFIX HAS TAKEN CHARGE OF ALL THE ATHLETES' TECHNICAL PROBLEMS.
WE MUST PLAN THEIR TRAINING CAREFULLY. FOREIGN FOOD COULD RUIN OUR CHAMPIONS' FITNESS.

WE MUST HAVE A WELL-BALANCED DIET.
WHAT **IS** A WELL-BALANCED DIET, O DRUID?

THAT IS!
13A

THE BARD CACOFONIX, IS PREPARING FOR THE POMP OF THE CEREMONIES.
I WILL NOW COMPOSE AN OLYMPIC HYMN.
!

NO, YOU ARE NOT GOING TO SING!
CLONK!

?
?
PAF!

WHAT'S THE MATTER WITH HIS HYMN?
I THINK HE'S SINGING FLAT.

AND THE DAY BEFORE SETTING OFF, THE ATHLETES DO THEIR PACKING.

13B

AT LAST THE DAY OF DEPARTURE DAWNS. OUR FRIENDS SET OFF FOR OLYMPIA AND OLYMPIC GLORY!
UP GAUL! WE ARE THE CHAMPIONS!
WOOF! WOOF! WOOF!

THAT'S STRANGE! I SUDDENLY FEEL THERE AREN'T MANY MEN AROUND HERE...

COME ALONG, LET'S MAKE THE MOST OF IT! WE CAN GET THE PLACE TIDIED UP A BIT BEFORE THOSE LOUDMOUTHS COME BACK!

ALL ABOARD! DON'T FORGET THE BOARS!

GOOD MORNING, CAPTAIN! DOES YOUR BOAT GO AT A GOOD RATE OF KNOTS?
THAT'S A KNOTTY QUESTION. IT'S UP TO YOU...

THERE ARE YOUR SEATS!
!?

WHAT ARE YOU MOANING ABOUT? ONE CLASS ONLY, AS AGREED. AS FOR DECK GAMES AND SPORT, YOU'RE GOING TO GET PLENTY OF THAT.

AND I ADVISE YOU TO GET ROWING, FOR A START. WE MUST SAIL WITH THE TIDE.

WHAT ABOUT THE ATMOSPHERE?
YOU HAVE A POINT THERE. LET THE MUSIC BEGIN!
SNAP

BONG!
BONG!

AND DON'T MAKE ANY FUSS. YOU'RE GETTING LUXURY CLASS. ON THE USUAL CRUISES, THE PASSENGERS ARE CHAINED UP AND WHIPPED. THERE'S A LONG WAITING LIST. EVERYONE WANTS TO GET TO THE OLYMPIC GAMES!
15A

THE GALLEY SETS OFF FOR ITS DISTANT DESTINATION, THE FASCINATING LAND OF GREECE, WITH ITS PASSENGERS IN THAT DELIGHTFUL SHIPBOARD MOOD WHICH MAKES YOU FORGET ALL YOUR WORRIES.
BOM! BOM! BOM! BOM! BOM! BOM! BOM!

THERE'S NOTHING LIKE A SEA VOYAGE TO RELAX YOU, IS THERE, ASTERIX?
NO, IT'S THE STOPS THAT ARE SO TIRING.

NOW AND THEN SOME INCIDENT OR CHANCE MEETING MAKES A PLEASANT CHANGE.

A PIRATE GALLEY!
WHERE?

GALLEY RIGHT AHEAD!

THERE AREN'T ONE OR TWO GAULS ABOARD THAT GALLEY, BY ANY CHANCE?

IT'S SWARMING WITH FEROCIOUS GAULISH WARRIORS!

NOW LET'S KEEP CALM, ME HEARTIES. WE'RE OUT OF OUR DEPTH HERE. STAND BY TO ABANDON SHIP! SCUTTLE HER!

THEY'RE OURS, AREN'T THEY, ASTERIX?
WOOF!
DON'T PUSH!
OLD PEOPLE FIRST!
JUST A MINUTE!
16A

?
?
BOARDING PIRATE VESSELS IS NOT INCLUDED IN THE FARE. IT'S AN EXTRA.

WHAT D'YOU MEAN, AN EXTRA?
I'D JUST LIKE TO POINT OUT THAT BOARDING IS AN OPTIONAL EXTRA ...

APPLY TO THE PURSER. IT'S TWO SESTERTII.

WE'LL COMPLAIN TO THE COMPANY! IT'S AN ABSOLUTE DISGRACE! YOU CAN KEEP YOUR BLESSED PIRATE!

BOM! BOM! BOM!BOM!
BOM!BOM!
WHAT ABOUT US, THEN? THEY REALLY ARE GETTING RATHER TIRESOME!
WHO'S FOR DINNER? SHALL WE DRAW LOTS, BOYS?
YOU'VE MANAGED TO KEEP YOUR PLACE IN THE SUN, I SEE!
16B

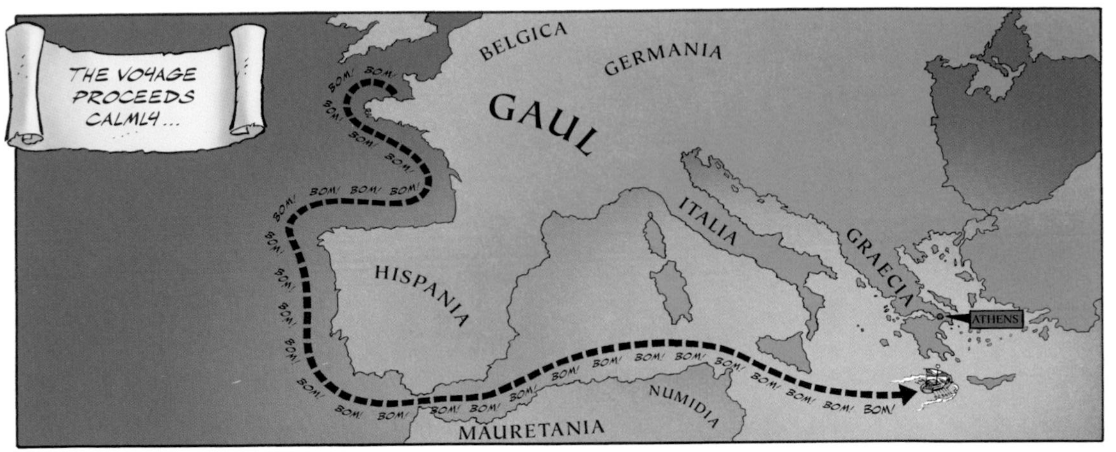
THE VOYAGE PROCEEDS CALMLY...
BELGICA
GERMANIA
GAUL
HISPANIA
ITALIA
GRAECIA
ATHENS
NUMIDIA
MAURETANIA
BOM! BOM!

...UNTIL AT LAST, ONE DAY...
WE'LL BE THERE TOMORROW, BOYS! PIRAEUS AWAITS US!

THAT'S FUNNY. I'D HAVE THOUGHT SOMEONE WOULD SAY SOMETHING, BUT I SUPPOSE IT'S ALL GREEK TO THEM.

GETAFIX...
YES?

WHO IS PIRAEUS?
AH! GOOD!

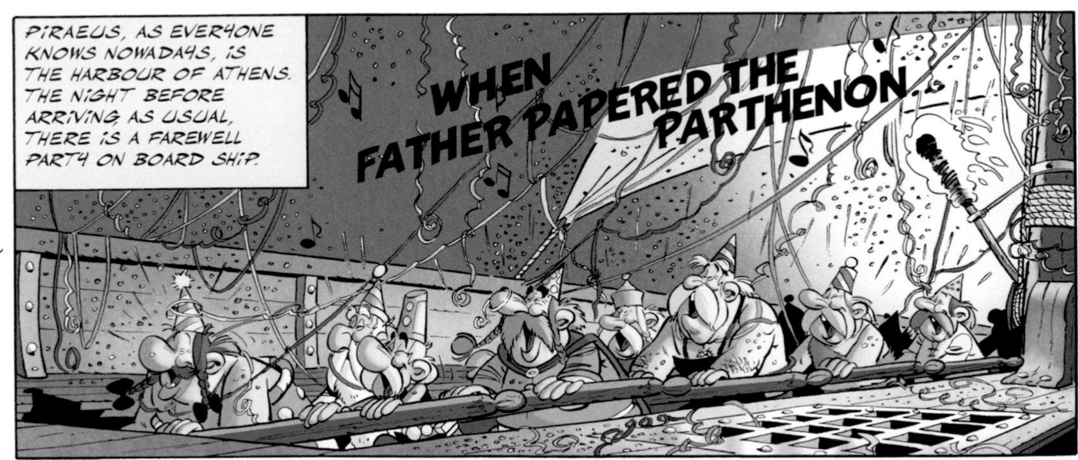
PIRAEUS, AS EVERYONE KNOWS NOWADAYS, IS THE HARBOUR OF ATHENS. THE NIGHT BEFORE ARRIVING, AS USUAL, THERE IS A FAREWELL PARTY ON BOARD SHIP.
WHEN FATHER PAPERED THE PARTHENON...

BONG!
BONG!

AND AT LAST...

RIGHT, BOYS! WE REPRESENT GAUL; LET US BE WORTHY OF HER! WE WON'T DRAW ATTENTION TO OURSELVES, OR MAKE FUN OF THE NATIVES, EVEN IF THEY DON'T HAVE ALL THE ADVANTAGES OF OUR GLORIOUS CULTURAL HERITAGE!

OFF WE GO! AND DON'T FORGET THE BOARS.

HEY, ASTERIX!
WHAT IS IT?

HAVE YOU SEEN THEIR PROFILES?
SSH, OBELIX. YOU'LL PUT THEIR NOSES OUT OF JOINT!

I AM DIABETES, A GUIDE. I CAN TAKE YOU TO ATHENS BY CHARIOT AND SHOW YOU ROUND THE CITY, IF YOU LIKE.
18A

WE'VE GOT A LITTLE TIME TO SPARE BEFORE WE LEAVE FOR OLYMPIA. IT WOULD BE A PITY NOT TO VISIT ATHENS.

SHALL WE GO BOYS?
YERRSS!
YOU CAN EXCHANGE YOUR SESTERTII FOR OBOLS, DRACHMAS AND MINES AT MAKALOS'S PLACE. YOU'RE QUITE SAFE; HE'S A COUSIN OF MINE.
?

YOU CAN FEEL QUITE SAFE WITH THE CHARIOT DRIVER TOO. HE'S KUDOS, ANOTHER COUSIN OF MINE.
JUST A MINUTE. SOMEONE'S MISSING.

TEEHEEHEE!

GERIATRIX!
ALL RIGHT, ALL RIGHT! THAT'S THE TROUBLE WITH THESE ORGANIZED TRIPS, YOU'RE NEVER FREE TO DO YOUR OWN THING!
18B

UP GAUL!
WE ARE THE CHAMPIONS!
GALLO-ROMAN TEAM

DON'T YOU THINK WE SHOULD ASK THEM TO BE A LITTLE QUIETER?
HUH! WE'RE GOING TO WIN THE GAMES, SO WE MAY AS WELL MAKE A SPLASH.

I'LL DRIVE YOU TO A GOOD HOTEL IN ATHENS. MY COUSIN PHALLINTODISEUS IS THE MANAGER.
THESE HORSES ARE GOOD.

YES, THEY'RE AN EXCELLENT TEAM... THEY'RE ALL COUSINS.

I'LL SHOW YOU THE ACROPOLIS!
NO, OBELIX, NOT ANOTHER COUSIN!
I DIDN'T SAY A WORD! WHO IS THIS THEA CROPOLIS?
THERE SHE IS!

ATHENS

IN A CHEAP ROOM AT A SMALL ATHENS HOTEL...
FOR JUPITER'S SAKE! STOP CARRYING ON LIKE THAT!

I'VE DECIDED TO SPEND A FEW DAYS HERE IN ATHENS, SO THAT YOU CAN GET YOUR MORALE BACK BEFORE JOINING UP WITH THE OTHER ROMAN ATHLETES AT OLYMPIA...
PARTHENON

YOU'RE RIGHT: I MUST TRY AND CALM DOWN.
THAT'S IT! FORGET ABOUT THOSE GAULS!

HOORAY! WE'RE HERE, BOYS!
HELLO? WHAT'S THAT NOISE?

LET'S SEE!

GALLO-ROMAN

WHAT IS IT?
MIND YOUR OWN BUSINESS! AND DON'T FORGET TO SWEEP OUT THE CORNERS!

YOU'LL BE VERY COMFORTABLE HERE, BY ZEUS. THE HOTEL IS VERY CROWDED, SO YOU'LL HAVE TO SHARE ROOMS.
WHAT ABOUT THE BOARS?

YOU CAN KEEP PETS IN YOUR ROOMS. WE HAVE TO PIG IT A BIT WHEN THE PLACE IS SO FULL.
OINK!

EXCEPT FOR THE BOARS, WHO ARE VERY FUSSY ANIMALS, EVERYONE IS VERY PLEASED WITH THE ACCOMMODATION.
I'M WARNING YOU, I SLEEP WITH THE WINDOW CLOSED!
OINK!

COME ALONG, BOYS! DIABETES IS GOING TO SHOW US THE ACROPOLIS.

AND SOON AFTERWARDS ALL OUR TRAVELLERS CAN BE SEEN ON THE SACRED ROCK OF THE ACROPOLIS, WHERE THEY ADMIRE THE PROPYLAEA, THE TEMPLE OF NIKE, AND THAT MASTERPIECE OF CLASSICAL ARCHITECTURE, THE PARTHENON...
IT REMINDS ME OF BURDIGALA...
NO, THERE'S A LITTLE SQUARE IN MASSILIA ...
WHAT, NO DOLMENS?
WHAT ARE **YOU** DOING HERE?
NOT BAD, IF YOU LIKE COLUMNS.
OINK!

LOOK AT THAT! LOOK AT THAT, MY FRIENDS!
SMASHING!

HOLD IT THERE!

WELL, WHAT D'YOU THINK OF IT?
MAGNIFICENT!
YES, IT'S QUITE GOOD, FOR FOREIGNERS.

21
SPEAKING OF FOREIGNERS, HERE COME OUR FELLOW COUNTRYMEN!
!

I AM NOT YOUR FELLOW COUNTRYMAN! IF I HAD MY WAY I'D GIVE YOU BACK GAUL AND REPATRIATE EVERYBODY!

BY TOUTATIS! IT OFFENDS MY ROMAN SPIRIT TO HEAR YOU TALK LIKE THAT!

SERIOUSLY, NOW. YOU'RE NEVER GOING TO TAKE PART IN THE GAMES?
WITH THE MAGIC POTION THAT MAKES US INVINCIBLE, YOU MUST ADMIT WE'D BE STUPID NOT TO!

BUT IT'S NOT FAIR! WHAT'S GOING TO BECOME OF US?

WE'RE NOT STOPPING YOU ENTERING... IT'S JUST THAT WE'RE GOING TO WIN...

...THAT'S THE POINT!

I'M TAKING YOU TO HAVE LUNCH AT MY COUSIN'S RESTAURANT. HIS NAME'S THERMOS.
THERE'S NO DEPOSIT ON THE AMPHORA. WHAT DO I DO WITH IT?
KEEP IT. IT'LL MAKE A NICE SOUVENIR.
OINK!

SO OUR TOURIST FRIENDS ARE INTRODUCED TO THE JOYS OF STUFFED VINE LEAVES, KEBABS, OLIVES, WATER-MELON AND RESINATED WINE.
IT'S NOT A PATCH ON BOAR!
OINK!
I HAD ONE WITH ME, BUT I LEFT HIM OUTSIDE. YOU'RE NOT SUPPOSED TO BRING YOUR OWN FOOD.
WHAT ON EARTH DO THEY PUT IN THEIR WINE?
OH, FOR A DROP OF AQUITANIAN WINE!
D'YOU REMEMBER THAT LITTLE RESTAURANT NEAR LUGDUNUM WHERE WE HAD THAT DELICIOUS VEAL?

THIS IS OUR LAST NIGHT IN ATHENS. DIABETES TOLD ME ABOUT A GOOD PLACE TO EAT. ONE OF HIS COUSINS IS THE MANAGER...

INVINOVERITAS
CLAP! CLAP! CLAP! CLAP! CLAP!
YAHOOO! YAHAAA!
THEY SEEM TO BE HAVING A GOOD TIME IN THERE!
THEY'RE FOND OF DANCING... I HEAR GREEK DANCES ARE VERY INTERESTING...

?
CLAP! CLAP!
CLAP! CLAP! CLAP!
CLACK! CLACK! CLACK!
CLAP!
CLAP! CLAP!

COME ON, BOYS! I'M GIVING THEM A DEMONSTRATION OF GAULISH DANCING!
TAP!
23A

AS THE NIGHT GOES ON, OUR FRIENDS ARE INTRODUCED TO THE ART OF GREEK DANCING...
LALA...
LALA...
LALA...
LALA...
LALA...
LALA...
CLOP! CLOP!

AND FINALLY...
COME ALONG, GERIATRIX. THE SUN WILL SOON BE RISING!
I *HIC!* ONE LAST HORN!

I FEEL *HIC!* TEN YEARS YOUNGER!
WELL, THAT MAKES YOU EIGHTY-THREE, AND IT'S TIME YOU WERE IN BED!

UP WITH THE GREEKS!
WHAT'S THAT?
I'LL GO AND SEE.

IT'S OUR OPPONENTS, TRAINING!
23B

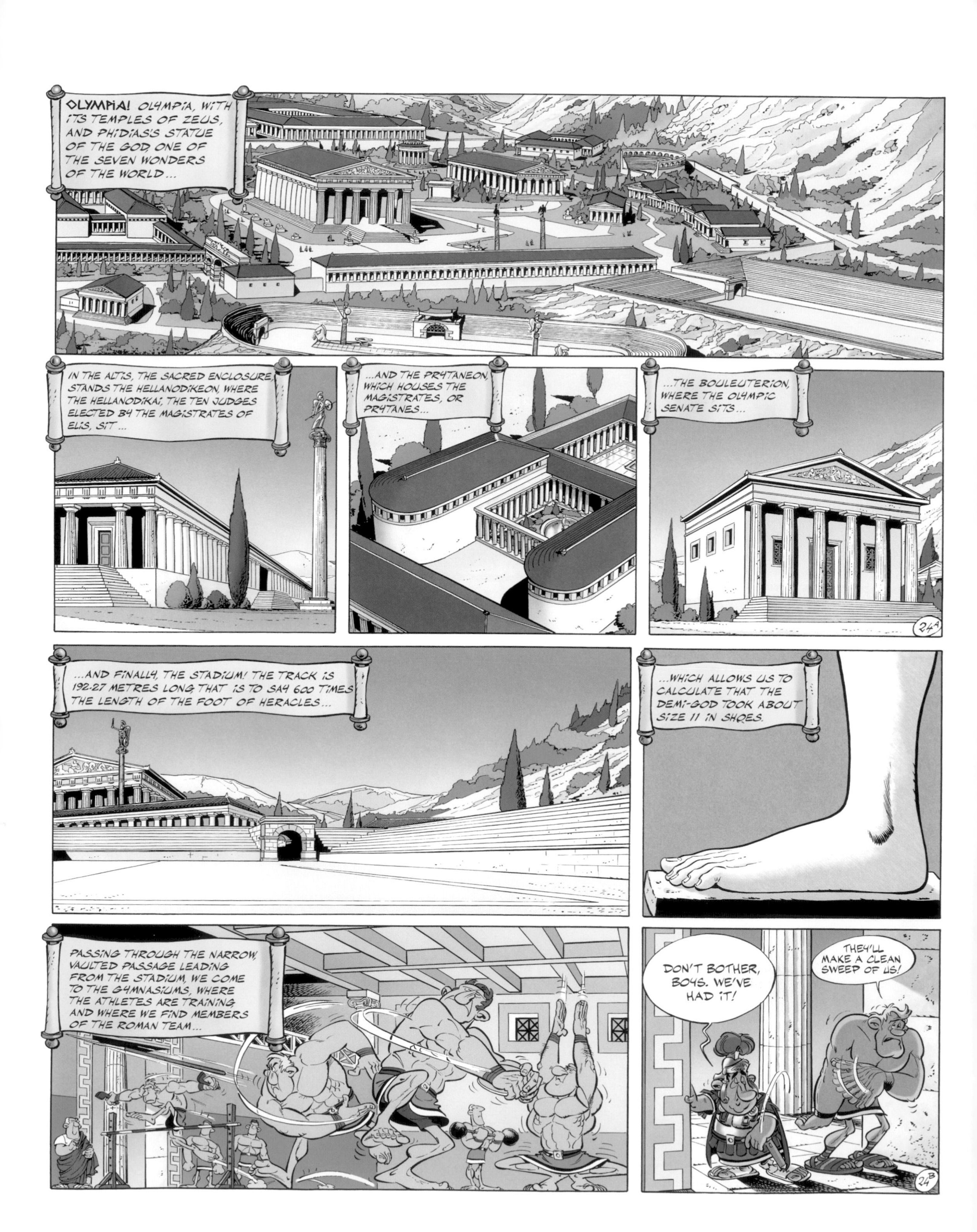
OLYMPIA! OLYMPIA, WITH ITS TEMPLES OF ZEUS, AND PHIDIAS'S STATUE OF THE GOD, ONE OF THE SEVEN WONDERS OF THE WORLD...
IN THE ALTIS, THE SACRED ENCLOSURE, STANDS THE HELLANODIKEON, WHERE THE HELLANODIKAI, THE TEN JUDGES ELECTED BY THE MAGISTRATES OF ELIS, SIT...
...AND THE PRYTANEON, WHICH HOUSES THE MAGISTRATES, OR PRYTANES...
...THE BOULEUTERION, WHERE THE OLYMPIC SENATE SITS...
...AND FINALLY, THE STADIUM! THE TRACK IS 192.27 METRES LONG, THAT IS TO SAY 600 TIMES THE LENGTH OF THE FOOT OF HERACLES...
...WHICH ALLOWS US TO CALCULATE THAT THE DEMI-GOD TOOK ABOUT SIZE 11 IN SHOES.
PASSING THROUGH THE NARROW, VAULTED PASSAGE LEADING FROM THE STADIUM, WE COME TO THE GYMNASIUMS, WHERE THE ATHLETES ARE TRAINING AND WHERE WE FIND MEMBERS OF THE ROMAN TEAM...
DON'T BOTHER, BOYS. WE'VE HAD IT!
THEY'LL MAKE A CLEAN SWEEP OF US!

WHILE THE GREEK ATHLETES ARE TRAINING ENERGETICALLY, UNDER THE VIGILANT EYE OF THEIR TRAINERS, THE ALIPTES...

...THE GAULS ARE HAVING A NAP BETWEEN MEALS...

...AND THE ROMANS HAVE GIVEN UP TRYING AS WELL AS HOPE ...
THERE IS A TABERNA IN THE TOWN...

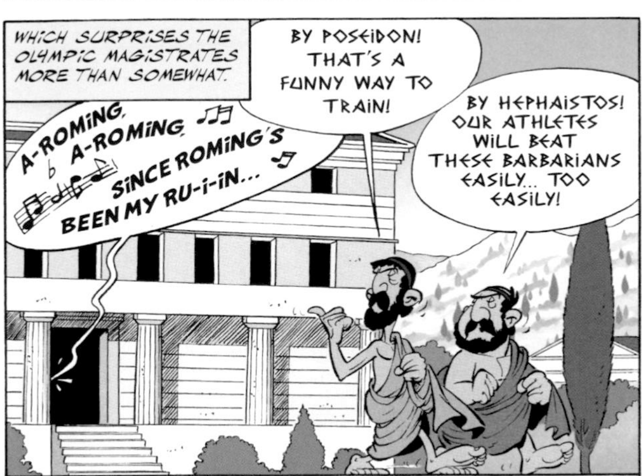

WHICH SURPRISES THE OLYMPIC MAGISTRATES MORE THAN SOMEWHAT.
A-ROMING, A-ROMING, SINCE ROMING'S BEEN MY RU-I-IN...
BY POSEIDON! THAT'S A FUNNY WAY TO TRAIN!
BY HEPHAISTOS! OUR ATHLETES WILL BEAT THESE BARBARIANS EASILY... TOO EASILY!

?!
?!

LOOK AT THAT! THEY'RE STUFFING THEMSELVES!
WHILE OUR VIRTUOUS ATHLETES ARE LIVING ON FIGS, OLIVES...

RAW MEAT AND WATER!

BUT THE GREEKS GET WIND OF SOMETHING...
SNIFF! SNIFF!

...WHICH LEADS TO REGRETTABLE INCIDENTS IN THE OLYMPIC VILLAGE.
I'M NOT EATING THIS!

WHAT DO YOU MEAN, YOU'RE NOT EATING THAT?
IT'S NASTY.

NASTY? BUT YOU'RE A SPARTAN! SPARTANS DON'T MIND HARDSHIP!
ALL RIGHT, SO BACK HOME IN SPARTA WE DO LIVE ON OLIVE STONES AND GRISTLE...

BUT BACK HOME IN SPARTA WE DON'T HAVE SAVAGES NEXT DOOR, STUFFING THEMSELVES WITH DELICIOUS THINGS ALL DAY LONG!

BUT THEY'RE DECLINING!
AND SUPPOSE I WANT TO DECLINE TOO, BY ARTEMIS!
THAT'S RIGHT! WE DECLINE!
WE DECLINE TO EAT THIS MUCK!
IF YOU WANT GAMES YOU'LL HAVE TO GIVE US BREAD!
AND KEBABS!
AND WINE!
HOW ABOUT A MAMMOTH STEAK?

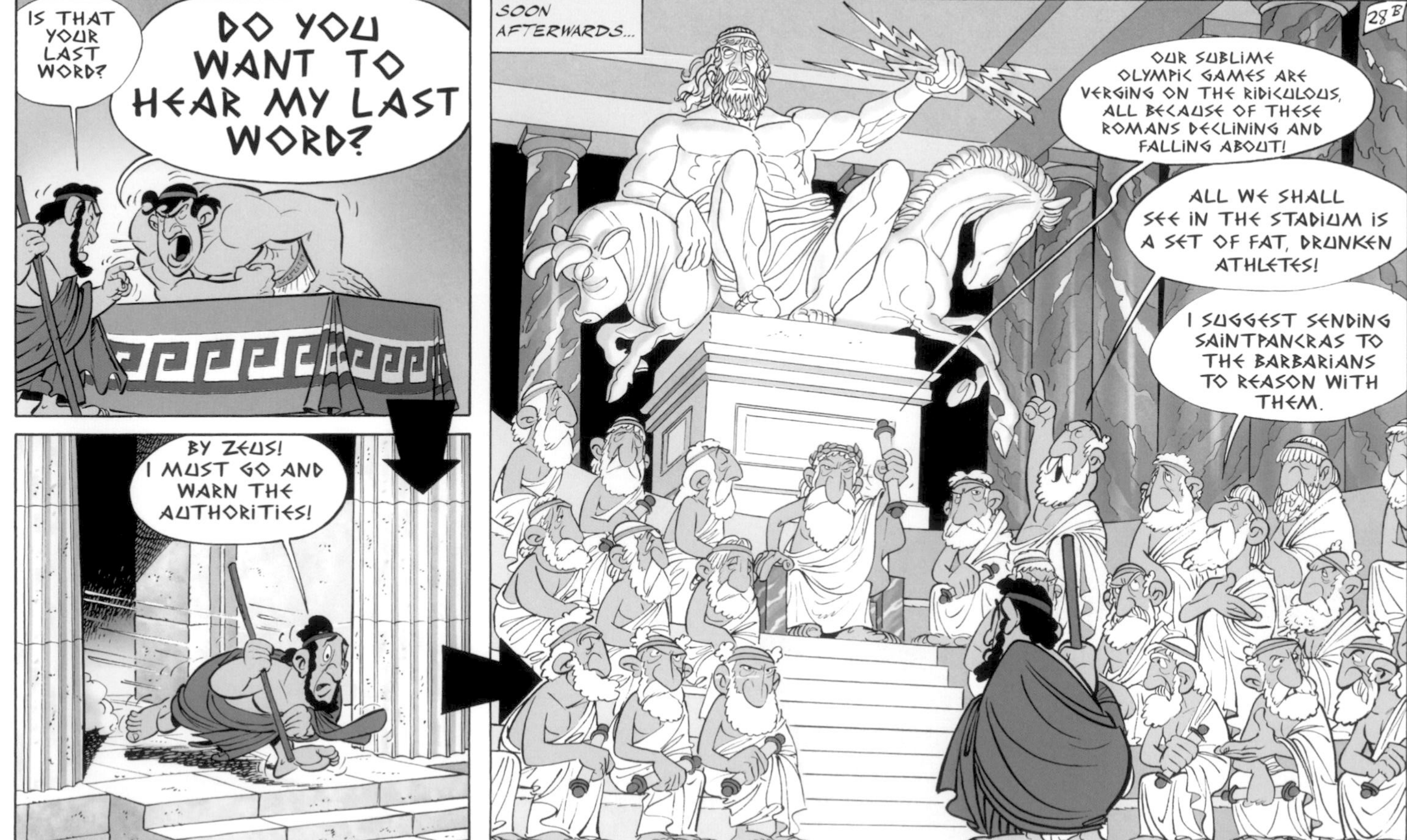

IS THAT YOUR LAST WORD?
DO YOU WANT TO HEAR MY LAST WORD?
BY ZEUS! I MUST GO AND WARN THE AUTHORITIES!
SOON AFTERWARDS...
OUR SUBLIME OLYMPIC GAMES ARE VERGING ON THE RIDICULOUS, ALL BECAUSE OF THESE ROMANS DECLINING AND FALLING ABOUT!
ALL WE SHALL SEE IN THE STADIUM IS A SET OF FAT, DRUNKEN ATHLETES!
I SUGGEST SENDING SAINTPANCRAS TO THE BARBARIANS TO REASON WITH THEM.

THIS IS WHERE THE ROMANS ARE TRAINING...

I AM SAINTPANCRAS, ONE OF THE OLYMPIC MAGISTRATES...
I SAY, A VISITOR! TAKE A COUCH, OLD MAN! THIRTY-ONE CAN FEAST AS CHEAPLY AS THIRTY!

AREN'T YOU ASHAMED OF YOURSELVES, ROMANS? WHAT WOULD JULIUS CAESAR SAY IF HE COULD SEE YOU?

HE WOULDN'T BE PLEASED, EH?

YOU MAY THINK WINE WILL INCREASE YOUR POWERS...
TEEHEEHEEHEE!
29A

BUT DON'T FORGET THE RULES; ALL ARTIFICIAL STIMULANTS ARE FORBIDDEN ON PENALTY OF DISQUALIFICATION!

THAT'SH RIGHT, THAT'SH RIGHT! CHEERSH!

PFFCHCH!

HEY, YOU! WAIT FOR ME, BY JUPITER!
?

SOON AFTERWARDS...
THERE THEY ARE!
?
?
29B

THAT'S THEM!

IS IT TRUE THAT YOU POSSESS A MAGIC POTION, AND YOU INTEND TO TAKE IT BEFORE THE GAMES?

YES, THAT'S RIGHT.

SUCH PROCEDURES ARE STRICTLY FORBIDDEN!

30A
STRICTLY?
STRICTLY!
STRICTLY.

ER... IN THE CIRCUMSTANCES, I'D LIKE TO APPLY FOR PERMISSION TO LEAVE THE SACRED ENCLOSURE AND CONSULT OUR FRIENDS.
GRANTED!

HO, HO, HO! I'M OFF TO GIVE THE OTHERS THE GOOD NEWS!

GET UP, EVERYONE! STAND TO ATTENTION! TO WORK! YOU BARBARIC LOT! GLUTEUS MAXIMUS! PULL YOUR SOCCI UP! AND JUMP TO IT!

BUT THIS IS ONLY THE EIGHTH COURSE...
SO MUCH FOR THE EIGHTH COURSE!

30B
AH, THE DISCOBOLI HAVE STARTED TRAINING AGAIN AT LAST.

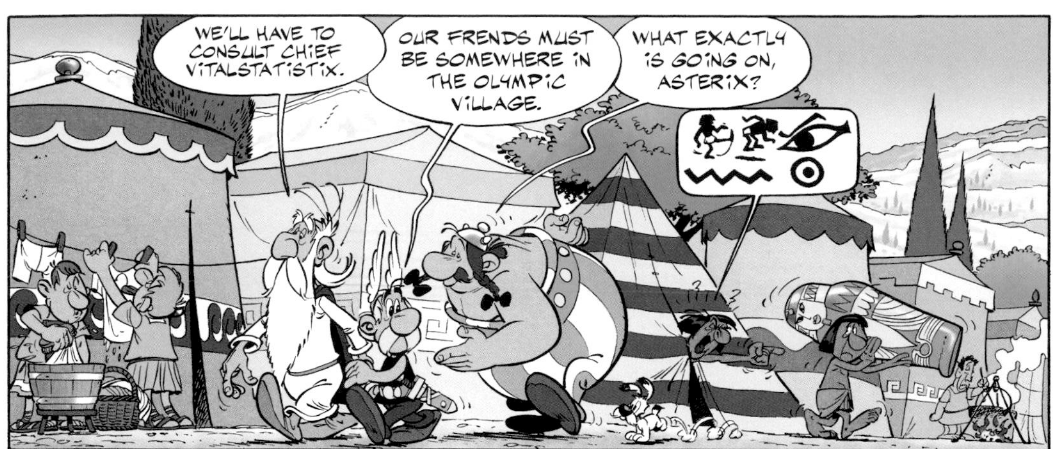

* THE BATTLE OF GERGOVIA, 52BC

OBELIX COULD COMPETE ON HIS OWN...
WHY ON MY OWN?

NO, NO! IT WOULDN'T BE FAIR.
WHAT WOULDN'T BE FAIR?

HE FELL INTO THE CAULDRON OF MAGIC POTION WHEN HE WAS A BABY...
!?!

JUST A MINUTE!

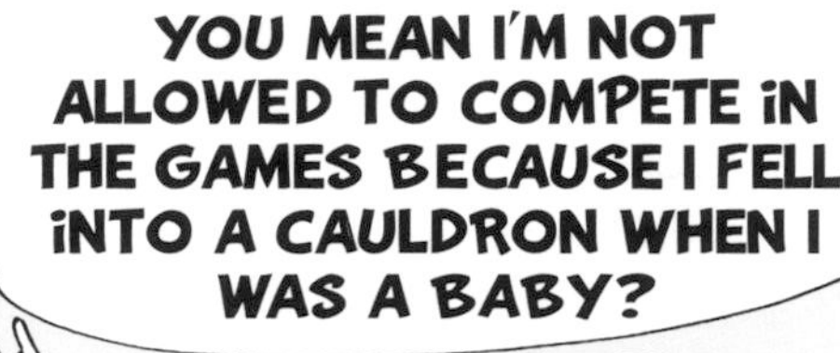
YOU MEAN I'M NOT ALLOWED TO COMPETE IN THE GAMES BECAUSE I FELL INTO A CAULDRON WHEN I WAS A BABY?

PRECISELY!
RIGHT! THAT WAS ALL I WANTED TO KNOW!

NO ONE EVER EXPLAINS ANYTHING TO ME.
?!

WELL, THEN, THIS IS WHAT WE'LL DO. WE KEEP ASTERIX ENTERED FOR THE GAMES. GETAFIX AND OBELIX WILL ACT AS HIS TRAINERS... AND WE MUST TRUST IN THE GODS!

HAVE NO FEAR, BOYS! WITH US TO CHEER HIM ON, ASTERIX CAN'T LOSE!
WON'T SOMEONE PLEASE MAKE HIM SHUT UP?

ONE PALM OF VICTORY WOULD DO... YOU'LL COMPETE ONLY IN THE TRACK EVENTS.
LET'S GET BACK TO THE ENCLOSURE, FAST. I'M IN A HURRY TO START TRAINING.

FUNNY, ALL THE SAME, THIS DISCRIMINATORY ANTI-POT RULE!

I'LL SPRINT ROUND THE TRACK. SAND ME, WILL YOU?

HMM... NOT BAD, BUT IS IT GOOD ENOUGH TO BEAT THOSE HIGHLY TRAINED ATHLETES?
HOW ABOUT USING FINER SAND?

LET'S GO TO BED. THE GAMES BEGIN TOMORROW ... I FEEL FULL OF CONFIDENCE!

AND HOW ABOUT TELLING THEM I FELL INTO AN AMPHORA INSTEAD OF A CAULDRON?

THAT NIGHT, IN THE SACRED ENCLOSURE, ALL THE ATHLETES DREAM OF HONOUR AND VICTORY...
II
I

I

II
I

THE GREAT DAY DAWNS! SPECTATORS ARRIVE FROM ALL OVER THE CIVILIZED WORLD ... MEN ONLY, FOR WOMEN ARE FORBIDDEN TO WATCH THE OLYMPIC GAMES.
ONE OF THESE DAYS YOU'LL SEE! WOMEN WILL TAKE PART IN THE GAMES! NOT JUST AS SPECTATORS, EITHER!
YES, AND I SUPPOSE THEY'LL BE DRIVING CHARIOTS TOO!

AH, HERE ARE OUR SEATS!

RIGHT! IT'S ALL SETTLED, THEN – WE ACT IN A CALM AND DIGNIFIED WAY AND RESPECT OUR OPPONENTS! WE'LL BE GOOD SPORTS AND NOT MAKE OURSELVES CONSPICUOUS.
AS IF WE WOULD!

UP GAUL!

AFTER TAKING THE OLYMPIC OATH ON THE ALTAR OF ZEUS HERKIOS...
WE ARE FREE MEN OF PURE HELLENIC BLOOD WHO HAVE NEVER COMMITTED ANY CRIMINAL OR SACRILEGIOUS ACTS. WE SWEAR TO ABIDE BY THE RULES OF THE GAMES...
34A

...THE ATHLETES ENTER THE STADIUM. THE MEN FROM THERMOPYLAE ARE THE FIRST TO PASS BY. EVERYONE IS BACK IN TRAINING; THE ATHLETES FROM MAGNESIA ARE ON A MILK DIET. THE TEAM FROM COS IS ON LETTUCE, AND EVEN THE MEN OF SALAMIS HAVE GONE VEGETARIAN...
THERMOPYLAE

...AND THERE IS A SPARTAN ASSORTMENT WHO ARE BAREFOOT. BUT A FEW OF THE ATHLETES ARE LATE; THE MARATHON TEAM HAS HAD TO COME A LONG DISTANCE, AND SOME OF THE COMPETITORS FROM ATTICA ARE MYSTERIOUSLY ELEUSIVE...
SPARTA

RHODES HAS SENT ONLY ONE REPRESENTATIVE, A COLOSSUS...
RHODES

YOOHOO! BIG BROTHER IS WATCHING YOU!
SSH! LET'S BE GOOD SPORTS!

...AND IF THE ROMAN TEAM AS A WHOLE IS RECEIVED WITH GENERAL INDIFFERENCE, THE SAME CANNOT BE SAID FOR ONE OF ITS MEMBERS.
34B
GAUL!
GAUL! GAUL!
AS-TER-IX!
AS-TER-IX!
HURRAH!
GAUL

* WE SEE HERE THE ORIGIN OF AN EXPRESSION WHICH HAS COME DOWN TO US FROM ANCIENT OLYMPIC TIMES.

WHILE THE WINNERS MOUNT THE PODIUM TO RECEIVE THEIR PALMS...
HOLD IT THERE!
I
II
III

...AND THE FANS MAKE THEIR OWN COMMENTS ...
THE TRACK'S SOFT.

THERE'S THE CLIMATE, TOO... IT'S A HARD CLIMATE!
AND DON'T FORGET THE ALTITUDE...
OR THE BOARS' FOOD. THE POOR CREATURES AREN'T USED TO...
AND THE ATTITUDE OF THE CROWD! IN MY DAY THEY SHOWED A BIT MORE RESTRAINT!

ONE EVENT FOLLOWS ANOTHER: ORDINARY WRESTLING ALL-IN WRESTLING BOXING...
CRACK!

IN THESE EVENTS NEUROSES, THE COLOSSUS OF RHODES, IS UNBEATABLE.
AHA!
AHA!
AHA!

FLATTEN HIM, OUR KID!
AHA!
AHA!
AHA!

ARE ALL YOUR FAMILY LIKE THAT?
OH NO! OUR ELDEST BROTHER IS MUCH STRONGER...

BUT HE COULDN'T COME. MUMMY HAD TO SMACK HIM, AND HE HASN'T GOT OVER IT YET. HA, HA, HA!

SPORT KEEPS YOU FIT, THEY SAID...
MENS SANA IN CORPORE SANO, THEY SAID...
I
II
III

AT THE END OF THE DAY, THE ATHLETES RETURN TO THE SACRED ENCLOSURE TO TAKE STOCK...
WELL, IN VIEW OF YOUR BRILLIANT RESULTS, DO YOU THINK JULIUS CAESAR IS GOING TO BE PLEASED?

IN THE BOULEUTERION, THE OLYMPIC SENATE, THE MAGISTRATES, HELLANODIKAI, PRIESTS AND OFFICIALS HAVE ASSEMBLED. PHILIBUSTER, THE GREAT ORATOR, IS IN THE CHAIR.
NOBLE AND VENERABLE FRIENDS! OUR OWN ATHLETES ARE GOING TO WIN ALL THE PALMS, AS USUAL!
THAT'S RIGHT!
BY ATHENE!
BY APOLLO!
UP WITH US!

NONE THE LESS, IF WE DON'T GIVE THESE ROMAN BARBARIANS THE CHANCE OF WINNING ONE PALM, TOURISTS WILL TAKE NO MORE INTEREST IN OUR GAMES...

AND AS MY COUSIN DIABETES PUTS IT: NO MORE TOURISTS, NO MORE MONEY, NO MORE BUSINESS! OUR BEAUTIFUL MONUMENTS WILL FALL INTO RUIN! NO ONE WILL EVER WANT TO LOOK AT THEM THEN!

BUT WE CAN'T ASK OUR ATHLETES TO CHEAT, JUST TO LET THESE DECADENT BARBARIANS WIN!

EUREKA! I THINK I HAVE IT!

ALL ROMANS ARE SUMMONED TO THE GYMNASIUM!
THAT'S US!
I'LL NEVER GET USED TO IT!
37

ROMANS! THE OLYMPIC SENATE HAS DECIDED TO FIX AN EXTRA EVENT TOMORROW! A RACE OF XXIV STADIA, FOR ROMANS ONLY!

GOOD LUCK, AND MAY THE LEAST HOPELESS MAN WIN!

WHAT A PITY YOU CAN'T TAKE A FEW DROPS OF MAGIC POTION BEFORE THE RACE!

MAGIC POTION? YOU MEAN THE POTION IN THE CAULDRON IN THE SHED OVER THERE...?
YES, OF COURSE... I MEAN THE MAGIC POTION!

THE CAULDRON IN THE SHED OVER THERE – THE SHED WITH THE DOOR THAT DOESN'T SHUT PROPERLY?
38A

YES, THE CAULDRON IN THE SHED OVER THERE WITH THE DOOR THAT DOESN'T SHUT PROPERLY, THE ONE THAT ISN'T GUARDED BY NIGHT... WOULD THAT BE THE ONE YOU'RE TALKING ABOUT, OBELIX?
ER... YES!

OH, BUT WE'RE NOT ALLOWED TO DRINK THE MAGIC POTION IN THE CAULDRON IN THE SHED OVER THERE...
...WITH THE DOOR THAT DOESN'T SHUT PROPERLY, THE ONE THAT ISN'T GUARDED BY NIGHT.
?

HO, HO, HO!
HEE, HEE, HEE!
WHAT'S GOING ON?

OBELIX, YOU'RE BRIGHTER THAN ANY OF US!
?

38B
YOU KNOW SOMETHING, DOGMATIX? SINCE ASTERIX AND GETAFIX TURNED ROMAN, THEY'VE BEEN CRAZY TOO!
TAP! TAP! TAP!
WOOF!

HERE, GLUTEUS MAXIMUS...

IF WE ARE TO BE PROMOTED, JULIUS CAESAR HAS TO BE PLEASED, AND IF JULIUS CAESAR IS TO BE PLEASED, YOU HAVE TO WIN THE RACE AND THE PALM OF VICTORY...

NOW I HAVE AN IDEA THERE MAY BE A SHED OVER THERE, WITH A DOOR WHICH DOESN'T SHUT PROPERLY, ONE THAT ISN'T GUARDED BY NIGHT, CONTAINING...

A CAULDRON OF MAGIC POTION!
SSSH!
CLAP

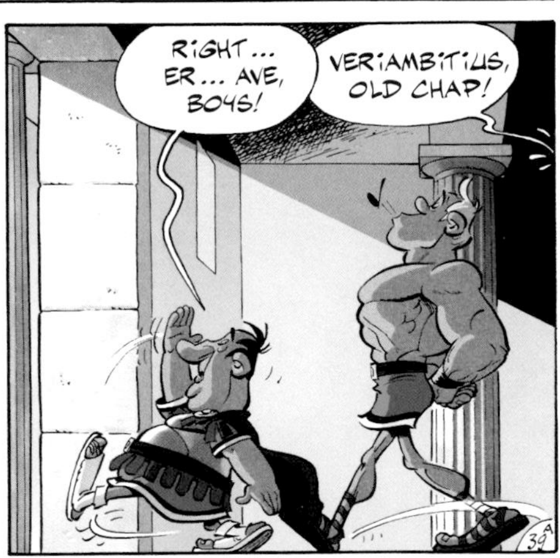
RIGHT... ER... AVE, BOYS!
VERIAMBITIUS, OLD CHAP!

QUO VADIS, VERIAMBITIUS? IT WILL SOON BE DARK. WE MUST GO TO BED EARLY, WITH THE RACE TOMORROW...
OH, WE WERE JUST OFF FOR A LITTLE WALK...

JULIUS CAESAR WOULDN'T BE VERY PLEASED TO KNOW THAT WE ROMANS WEREN'T STICKING TOGETHER...

WOULD HE?

AND THAT NIGHT...
?
ZZZZZZZ
ZZZZZZ
ZZZZZ

GRRRRRR!

?
GRRRRRR!

HEY! DOGMATIX HAS JUST WOKEN ME UP! THERE ARE LOTS OF PEOPLE PROWLING OVER THERE, BY THE SHED WITH THE DOOR WHICH DOESN'T SHUT PROPERLY, THE ONE THAT ISN'T GUARDED BY NIGHT, CONTAINING THE CAULDRON OF MAGIC POTION...

DOGMATIX IS A GREAT WATCHDOG!
WELL, YOU TELL YOUR GREAT WATCHDOG TO GO BACK TO SLEEP, AND MIND YOUR OWN BUSINESS!

BUT THEY MIGHT STEAL THE CAULDRON!

THEFT OF CAULDRONS IS NOT A CRIME AMONG THE HELLENES.
?!
40A

DO YOU UNDERSTAND ANYTHING AT ALL ABOUT THE CAULDRON LAWS IN THESE PARTS, DOGMATIX?

THESE HELLENES ARE CRAZY!

COCKADOODLEDOS

IT IS THE DAY OF THE 24 STADIA RACE, I.E. 4,614 METRES, 48 CENTIMETRES, OR AS WE MIGHT PUT IT MORE SIMPLY TODAY, 14,400 SIZE 11 SHOES LAID END TO END.
ALL COMPETITORS ON THE STARTING GROOVES!
40B

TEEHEEHEE!
SSH!
THESE BARBARIANS LOOK VERY SURE OF THEMSELVES!
I DARE SAY! WE'LL SEE WHAT'S LEFT OF THEIR CIVILIZATION IN A FEW YEARS' TIME!

O DRUID! I SUDDENLY HAD THE IDEA OF TAKING A LOOK AT THE SHED OVER THERE, THE ONE WITH THE...
YES, YES, I KNOW!

YES, BUT THE CAULDRON IS EMPTY!
OBELIX, THIS IS NO TIME TO BOTHER US! GO AND SIT IN THE STANDS WITH THE OTHERS!

OH, ALL RIGHT, I SEE! COME ON, DOGMATIX! ALL THE SAME, THEY COULD REALLY DO WITH SOMEONE BRIGHT HERE!

NO, YOU CAN'T SIT THERE; I'M KEEPING IT FOR MY BROTHER!
41A

THIS SEAT IS NOT TAKEN AND I'M IN NO MOOD FOR FOOLING ABOUT!
YOU'RE NOT HAVING THIS SEAT!

BIFF!

OH, AREN'T I, BY TOUTATIS!
?!

HAVE YOU SEEN MY BROTHER?
?!

YOU'RE A GLUTTON FOR PUNISHMENT, AREN'T YOU?
?

CLONK!
41B

READY?
I'LL SAY!
TEEHEEHEE!
WELL, WHAT ABOUT IT, BY JUPITER?

GET SET! GO!
THEY'RE OFF!

IN THE STANDS, THE ENTHUSIASM...
UP GAUL!
AS-TER-IX! AS-TER-IX!
COME ON, TITCH!
IF THEY ONLY KNEW... BUT NO ONE EVER LISTENS TO ME!

...IS BEYOND BELIEF!
AHA, AHA, AHA!

BUT THE RACE SOON TAKES A STRANGE TURN...

THE TRACK REALLY IS SOFT!
ASTERIX MUST HAVE EATEN A BOAR WHICH MUST HAVE EATEN SOMETHING...

THIS IS ALL TOPSY-TURVY!

...FOR ONE OF THE COMPETITORS IS ABOUT TO BE LAPPED BY ALL THE OTHERS, AN UNHEARD OF EVENT!
BRRROOOM!

THEY REACH THE FINISHING LINE!
!
GNGNGNGN!

IT MUST BE THEIR HABIT OF MARCHING IN RANKS, BY APOLLO!
HOW ARE WE GOING TO GET ALL THIS LOT ON THE PODIUM BY ARTEMIS?

CAESAR WILL BE PLEASED, WON'T HE?
ONE MOMENT! I WISH TO RAISE AN OBJECTION.
OBJECTION?

YES! THE TRACK WAS TOO SOFT!
AND THE BOARS AREN'T WELL EITHER; THEY MUST HAVE BEEN MAKING PIGS OF THEMSELVES!
43A

I ACCUSE ALL WHO FINISHED FIRST OF BEING FULL OF MAGIC POTION UP TO THE EARS!
THIS IS A VERY SERIOUS ACCUSATION! CAN YOU PROVE IT?

QUID?
QUOMODO?
THIS IS AN OUTRAGE!
I REFUSE TO SUBMIT TO...
CHEATS!
YAAAH!

YAAAH YOURSELF!

43B
LOOK! I ADDED SOME PERMITTED COLOURING MATTER TO THE CAULDRON OF MAGIC POTION... THOSE WHO DRANK IT HAVE ALL GOT BLUE TONGUES!
BY HERMES, YOU'RE RIGHT!

WE OUGHT TO HAVE HELD OUR TONGUES!
I'M FEELING RATHER BLUE MYSELF!
THE OLYMPIC SENATE WILL CONSIDER THIS UNPRECEDENTED SITUATION!
WINK! WINK!

A FEW MINUTES LATER...
ALL COMPETITORS WHO DRANK THE MAGIC POTION ARE DISQUALIFIED! THE PALM OF VICTORY IS THEREFORE AWARDED TO... ASTERIX!

ASTERIX! HURRAH FOR ASTERIX!
I ALWAYS KNEW THE LITTLE FELLOW HAD IT IN HIM!
YOU MEAN ... ASTERIX HAS WON?
IN A WAY, OBELIX, IN A WAY!
I SHOULD NOW LIKE ...

THE CROWD GOES WILD WITH ENTHUSIASM, AND IT IS ON THIS NOTE...
AHA, AHA, AHA!

...THAT WE LEAVE THE LAND OF THE HELLENES. OUR FRIENDS HAVE A QUIET CRUISE HOME...
I'VE GOT THAT SINKING FEELING AGAIN...
BOM! BOM! BOM! BOM!

...TO THEIR LITTLE VILLAGE, WHERE UNDER A STARRY SKY, THEY CELEBRATE THEIR OLYMPIC VICTORY – SOMETHING THAT DOES A LOT FOR ANY NATION'S PRESTIGE.
WHAT PUZZLES ME IS THE WAY THEY DISCRIMINATE AGAINST CAULDRONS...
EAT UP, DO, OBELIX!
AS FOR THE GREEK GIRLS, MY DEAR FELLOW – ABSOLUTELY STATUESQUE!
WHERE'S YOUR PALM OF VICTORY, ASTERIX?
DON'T TELL THE OTHERS, BUT I GAVE IT TO SOMEONE WHOSE NEED WAS GREATER THAN MINE, BY TOUTATIS!

AND FOR ONCE... FOR ONCE CAESAR IS PLEASED!
44
LEGIONARY GLUTEUS MAXIMUS, I MAKE YOU A CENTURION! CENTURION GAIUS VERIAMBITIUS, I PROMOTE YOU TO TRIBUNE!
THE END
-UDERZO- & GOSCINNY